FRED BOWEN
SPORTS STORY series

FRED BOWEN

PEACHTREE
ATLANTA

CONCORDIA UNIVERSITY LIBRARY
PORTLAND, OR 97211

Ω

Published by
PEACHTREE PUBLISHERS
1700 Chattahoochee Avenue
Atlanta, Georgia 30318-2112
www.peachtree-online.com

Text © 2010 by Fred Bowen

All rights reserved. No part of this publication may be reproduced, stored in
a retrieval system, or transmitted in any form or by any means—electronic,
mechanical, photocopy, recording, or any other—except for brief quotations in
printed reviews, without the prior permission of the publisher.

ISBN 978-1-56145-540-9 / 1-56145-540-7

Cover design by Maureen Withee and Thomas Gonzalez
Book design and composition by Melanie McMahon Ives
Manufactured in the United States of America
10 9 8 7 6 5 4 3 2 1
First Edition

Library of Congress Cataloging-in-Publication Data is available from the
Library of Congress

*To the memory of Brendan Ogg,
a young poet and writer who—
if he had been given more time—
would have written more books.*

Chapter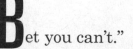

Bet you can't."

"Bet you I can." Jack Lerner and three of his friends walked swiftly through the Landon Middle School spring fair. The sun was shining and the parking lot was crowded with kids and their families.

Jack led the way past the moon bounce, the plant sale, the used-book sale, and a roped-off section where members of the band were painting little kids' faces.

"So where's the baseball booth?" Jack asked, looking around. "I want to see how fast I can throw." He was taller than his friends—all eighth graders at Landon—and his long stride kept him out in front.

"In the games section, near the basketball courts," said Danny Cruz, Jack's best buddy. "You can't miss it."

"You only have three chances to throw 75 miles an hour," said Jaylin Jackson. "It's not so easy."

Jack didn't say anything. He kept walking, fast.

"I bet Jack can throw at least that fast," Danny said, scrambling to catch up.

"No way," Annie Li said. "I pitch softball and I throw about 50 miles an hour. That's pretty fast."

"So what?" Danny said. "You're not the best athlete in the school like Jack here."

Jack smiled to himself as his friend continued to brag about him.

"He set the record in the softball throw and the rope climb last fall," Danny pointed out to no one in particular. "He even won the Ping-Pong tournament."

"Yeah, but 75 miles an hour? That's almost as fast as major league pitchers," Jaylin said.

By now Jack was several strides ahead of

his friends, but he could still hear them arguing.

"Jack struck out almost everybody in our league with his fastball last year," Danny insisted.

"But that was from 46 feet," Jaylin said. "We're in the Rising Stars League now. He's got to throw from 60 feet 6 inches this year."

Jack stopped at the edge of the games section and turned around to face his friends. "Okay, so Danny and I say I can do it," Jack said. He pointed at Jaylin and Annie. "And you guys say I can't."

"Right." Jaylin and Annie nodded.

"So what are we betting?" Jack asked with a confident smile. He glanced at the two long tables covered with plates of cookies, cakes, and brownies for the bake sale. His mouth was already starting to water. "How about if I throw one at seventy-five," he said, "you guys have to buy me and Danny some cookies or brownies?"

"Good idea," Danny said, licking his lips. "I'll take cookies *and* brownies."

"And if you *don't* throw 75 miles per hour,"

Annie added, "you guys have to buy me and Jaylin the cookies and brownies."

"Right." Jack thrust out his hand. "Deal?"

Jaylin and Annie suddenly looked less sure. "Wait a minute," Jaylin said. "You can't get, like, a million cookies."

"Just a bag," Jack said. "They only cost a buck."

Jaylin and Annie glanced at each other.

"Come on," Jack said, getting impatient. "The money goes to the school anyway."

"Okay, it's a deal." The four friends shook hands. Jack headed toward the baseball-toss booth, and the others trailed along behind him.

On the edge of the parking lot, a ten-foot-high green canvas was stretched between two metal poles. The white outline of a batter holding a bat had been painted on the canvas. To the side of the canvas, something that looked like a camera had been set up on a tripod.

"That's the speed gun," Danny said, pointing. "It tells you how fast the pitch is."

"Duh," said Annie.

A couple of grown-ups and one kid were already in line, waiting their turns. Jack began to windmill his left arm. "I better warm up," he said. "Hey, Danny, have you got a ball?"

Danny looked at the man taking tickets at the booth. "Can we borrow a baseball?"

"Sure." The man pulled a baseball from the bag tied to his waist and tossed it to Danny. "But bring it back when you're done."

"Wait a minute," Annie said to Jack. "We didn't say you could warm up." She held up three fingers. "Three throws," she said. "That was the bet."

"Are you kidding me?" Jack exclaimed. "I've got to warm up. I don't want to hurt my arm."

"It's okay," Jaylin assured Annie. "He's pitching in our first game on Tuesday. We'd better let him warm up."

"Yeah," Jack said. "Coach Bentley would kill us if I got hurt messing around right before the season."

After a few easy tosses, Jack got in line. The tall, lean man in front of him took a baseball and got ready to take his last turn.

"He looks like a decent athlete," Jaylin whispered to Jack. "He should be able to throw pretty hard."

"We'll see," Jack replied.

The man wound up and hurled the ball at the canvas. The ball landed with a *thud!* Jack and his friends all turned to check the small box that flashed the pitch speed in large, red numbers.

67

"Looks like the speed gun's a little slow," Danny said. "I thought that throw might hit at least seventy."

"The gun seems okay to me." Annie smiled.

The tall man stepped away and Jack handed over his ticket for three baseballs.

"Looks like we have a real major leaguer here...and he's a lefty, too," said the man in charge. "Okay, kid, let's see your best fastball."

Jack went into his windup. His left arm whipped by his ear and the ball smacked against the canvas with the same explosive *thud*.

Jack looked at the box.

70

"Whoa!" the man said, his head snapping back in surprise. "Seventy. That's the fastest pitch I've seen all day."

"Not fast enough," Jaylin muttered.

Jack grabbed the second ball. This time he reached back for a little something extra and let the ball rip.

Thud!

He quickly checked the speed box.

72

"Wow!" the man shouted. "This kid can really bring the heat."

"Still not fast enough," Annie said.

"He's got one more ball," Danny reminded everyone. "Come on, Jack, give it everything you got."

Jack tossed the final baseball up and down a couple times and took a few deep breaths. Finally, he wound up and threw with every ounce of his strength.

Thwack! The ball smacked the canvas like a clap of thunder.

75

"Oh, no! I can't believe it!" Jaylin shouted.

"I told you he could do it," Danny said. "Take it from me, he's gonna strike out everybody on Tuesday."

Jack just smiled. "Now how about those cookies?" he said, turning toward his friends. "I'm feeling kind of hungry."

Chapter 2

C ome on, Jack," Coach Bentley called from the bench. "Just put it over the plate!"

Jack stood on the pitcher's mound as a cool April breeze swept across the baseball diamond. *No kidding,* he thought. *I'm trying to throw strikes.*

Jack had walked two batters and struck out two in the first inning. Runners stood at first and second. Jack focused on Danny's mitt as he went into his windup and threw another fastball. It was high and wide.

"Ball three!" the umpire shouted. "Three balls, no strikes."

Jack slapped his glove against his leg. *Come on,* he told himself. *Throw your fastball right by the guy. Just like last season.*

The infielders for the Landon Bears kept up their chatter.

"Nothing but strikes, Jack."

"Right down the middle."

"You can do it."

Jack tried sizzling another fastball. The batter never moved.

"Ball four." The umpire signaled the batter to take his base.

Jack pounded his fist into his glove as each runner advanced. The bases were loaded.

Coach Bentley held up his hand. "Time," he said and walked slowly to the mound. "How are you doing?" he asked Jack.

"Okay," Jack said, twisting the ball in his hand.

"You only need one more out to end the inning. Just throw the ball across the plate. If he hits it, your fielders will make the play." Coach Bentley eyed the infielders who had gathered around the mound. "Be ready. We've got to get this batter!"

"Come on, Jack." Jaylin, the Bears shortstop, patted him on the back with his glove.

"You can do it. Put it right in there—75 miles an hour, just like that last pitch at the fair."

Jack steered the next pitch over the heart of the plate.

Smack! The batter hit a hard grounder toward shortstop. Jaylin took a short step left and scooped up the ball, but he bobbled it. He quickly grabbed it from the dirt with his bare hand and threw low to first base. The ball skipped by the Bears' first baseman and bounced to the fence.

"Back up home plate!" Coach Bentley yelled.

Jack dashed behind the plate and watched helplessly as three runners streaked across. It was the first inning of the first game of the season, and the Bears were behind 3–0.

He struck out the next batter with three blazing fastballs and ran off the mound. Tossing his glove into the dugout, he angrily kicked the dirt as Coach Bentley called out the batting order for the bottom of the first.

"Jaylin, Max, Danny. Come on, we need some hits. Let's get those runs back."

Jack slumped on the bench next to Annie,

who was keeping the Bears scorebook. "Not a great start," Jack muttered.

"Three walks in an inning is never good," Annie said.

"Jaylin should've made that play," Jack said in a low voice. "I should've been out of the inning without any runs."

Annie shrugged. "Yeah," she said. Then she looked back at the scorebook, tapping it with her pencil. "You threw thirty pitches, seventeen strikes and thirteen balls. You've got to do better than that."

But the next two innings were not much better. Jack threw hard and fast, but the ball kept sailing away from the plate. He was having a lot of trouble throwing strikes. He tried to focus on home plate, but Danny's catcher's mitt began to look smaller and smaller until it almost disappeared in the gray April afternoon.

Jack gave up three more walks and three more runs. The Bears were behind 6–2 after three innings. *This is definitely harder than last year,* he thought.

Coach Bentley walked down the bench

and stood in front of Jack. "I'm going to bring in Max Pickman to pitch," he said. "Annie says you've already thrown seventy-five pitches. That's a lot." He patted Jack on the shoulder. "I don't like to keep any pitcher in for much more than seventy pitches. And I don't want to use you all up in one game." He smiled. "It was a tough day to pitch. You did a good job. You just have to throw a few more strikes."

Jack buttoned his baseball jacket up to his neck. The day was getting colder. He sat helplessly at the end of the bench, watching his team go down to a 9–5 defeat. *I've got to throw more strikes,* he thought, digging his cleats deeper and deeper into the dirt. *But how?*

* * *

After the game, Jack sat in the backseat of the family minivan as his parents drove home.

"Tough game," his father observed.

"Yeah," Jack said.

"How does your arm feel?" his mother asked.

"Okay."

Jack wasn't in the mood for talking, especially to his parents. His mother and father were not really sports fans. They didn't know much about baseball or pitching. They had a lot more in common with his older sister Sarah, who taught English at a nearby high school.

"Danny had a nice hit," his mother said.

"Yeah."

Just then, his mother's cell rang.

Jack gazed out the back window, reviewing in his mind every pitch of his first loss. So many of them had sailed high and out of the strike zone. He only half-listened to his mother's conversation.

"Oh, good. It'll be great to see you," she was saying. "We could have lunch or dinner.... Okay, how about two o'clock Sunday?... So where did you meet him?... Right. We'll see you both on Sunday, then."

Mrs. Lerner clicked off the call and looked at Jack's dad. "That was Sarah. She wants us to meet her new boyfriend."

Mr. Lerner glanced over, taking his eyes off the road for a second. "Really? Who is it?" He sounded surprised.

"His name is Finn Riley," Mrs. Lerner said. "She said she met him a few weeks ago."

"Did she say what he does?"

"No, but he sounds nice." Mrs. Lerner turned in her seat toward Jack. "It'll be fun for all of us to meet him, won't it?"

Jack didn't answer. *Great,* he thought. *Another one of Sarah's geeky boyfriends. Who cares?* He kept looking out the window and going over the game, pitch by pitch. There was only thing he cared about right now.

Throwing more strikes.

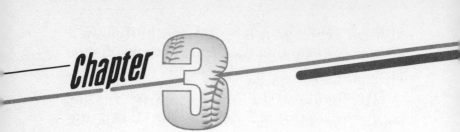

Chapter 3

They're here!" Mrs. Lerner called out in an excited voice. She checked her hair in the hall mirror and walked quickly to the front door.

Jack didn't move from the living room chair where he was reading *Sports Illustrated*. He glanced into the dining room. The table was set with nice plates, special glasses, and cloth napkins. *What's the big deal?* he wondered. *It's just another one of Sarah's boyfriends. It's not like it's Thanksgiving or anything.*

Sarah, petite with shoulder-length brown hair, walked through the door and hugged her parents. Strikeout, the family's terrier, barked excitedly. Jack got up and moved slowly toward them as Sarah took off her jacket.

"How's my little brother?" she asked, her blue eyes sparkling. "Or should I say, my *younger* brother? You're taller than I am now."

Jack gave Sarah a quick hug. She turned and extended an arm. "I want you all to meet a good friend of mine," she said. "Finn Riley."

Finn shook hands with everyone. "Hi, Jack," he said with a smile. "Sarah has told me a lot about you."

His handshake was firm and strong. He was tall, maybe more than six feet. He seemed more athletic than the other guys Jack's sister had brought home.

"I hope you're hungry," Mrs. Lerner said. "We have lots to eat."

Jack did more eating than listening after they sat down at the table. Mostly his mom and dad bombarded Sarah with questions about her classes. This was her first year of teaching at Leonardtown High School. Then Jack's dad turned to Finn.

"So what do you do, Finn?"

"I work at the high school with Sarah, Mr. Lerner."

"Are you a teacher?"

"No, I—"

Sarah interrupted. "Finn is one of the security people," she said. "That's how we met."

"Oh?" Mrs. Lerner sounded surprised.

"What kind of security do you do at the school?" Mr. Lerner asked.

"I make sure the kids are in class," Finn explained. "I monitor the parking lot, have lunch duty, that sort of thing."

Sarah smiled. "Finn has another job, too."

Mrs. Lerner leaned forward. "Oh, and what is that?"

"I'm the pitching coach and recruiting coordinator at Westminster College," Finn said.

Jack looked up from his plate. "Really?" he blurted out. "That's cool."

"Finn wants to be a head baseball coach at a college someday," Sarah added.

"So is the coaching only a part-time job?" Mr. Lerner asked.

Finn laughed. "It's full-time as far as the hours go. But it doesn't pay much so I have to work at the high school to pay my bills."

"Westminster won two games yesterday," Sarah said proudly. "And Finn's pitchers were great."

"You went to the baseball games?" her mother asked, sounding even more surprised. Sarah had never been that into sports.

"Well, I went to one of them," Sarah said.

Jack finally got a word in. "So did you play baseball?" he asked Finn.

Finn turned to Jack and smiled. "Sure, I played at Blair High School," he said. "And then I pitched four years at Macalester College in Minnesota."

"Finn was an All-Conference pitcher," Sarah said.

"Honorable mention All-Conference," Finn corrected with a grin.

"How fast did you throw?" Jack asked.

Finn looked around the table. "Not that hard," he said. "Maybe around 80 miles per hour."

"That's all?" Jack said, a bit disappointed.

"I didn't try to overpower the batters. I fooled them," Finn said. "I was one of those lefty pitchers who had a decent curveball and a real good changeup."

"Well, 80 miles per hour sounds fast to me," Mrs. Lerner said.

"I threw a pitch 75 miles an hour at the school fair last Sunday," Jack said.

"Really?" Finn said.

"Jack's a left-handed pitcher, too," Mr. Lerner said. "He was the starter for his team's season opener Tuesday."

"Maybe I should put you on the list of kids I'm recruiting." Finn smiled. "How'd you do on Tuesday?"

"Not so great." Jack shrugged. "We lost 9–5."

"How'd you do pitching?" Finn asked.

"Well, I gave up six runs in three innings," Jack answered. "But a bunch of those runs were unearned," he added quickly.

"Jack has to throw a few more strikes," Mr. Lerner said. "He gave up some walks."

Finn nodded as if he understood.

Sarah looked at her mother. "Finn gives

pitching lessons," she said. "It's another way for coaches to make some extra money."

Mr. Lerner leaned back from the table. "Maybe you can give Jack a couple of lessons, Finn. Get him to throw a few more strikes."

"We'd be happy to pay you," Mrs. Lerner said.

Finn held up his hands. "Oh, I couldn't accept money, Mrs. Lerner," he protested. "Especially after such a wonderful lunch." Then he looked at Jack. "I've got my baseball stuff in the car. We could play catch if you want. Or I could look at your pitching motion."

"That's very nice of you." Mrs. Lerner beamed.

Mr. Lerner pushed back from the table. "How about it, Jack? Want to have a real college coach take a look at you?"

"Sure!" Jack blurted out. "I'll give Danny a call and see if he'll come over and catch."

He couldn't believe his good luck. Finn wasn't just a baseball coach. He was a pitching coach. And a lefty. *This guy is perfect,* Jack thought.

J ack stood in the middle of a lumpy infield in back of Cloverly Elementary, the school around the corner from his house. He was dressed in sweatpants, a baseball practice shirt with long blue sleeves, and a Landon baseball hat. Behind home plate— 60 feet and 6 inches away—Danny waited in front of a chain-link backstop.

Finn stood next to Jack with a plastic bucket filled with baseballs. He had on his dark blue Westminster baseball hat and wraparound sunglasses. After a game of catch to warm up, Finn flipped Jack a base-ball from the bucket. "Okay, let's see what you've got."

Jack wound up and threw hard. The ball

whistled through the spring sunshine toward the plate. Danny reached up and away from the plate to snag the ball.

"That must have been at least seventy-five," Danny said. He tossed the ball to the side and got ready for another pitch.

Jack turned to see if Finn had been impressed with the speed of his fastball. But Finn just tossed him another baseball. "Go ahead. Do it again," he said, motioning with his chin toward home plate. "I want to watch your pitching motion."

Jack threw several more pitches, each as fast as the one before. But most of them flew high and out of the strike zone. Finn stood still and silent, with his arms crossed and the sun reflecting off his glasses. His face held no hint of expression.

After Jack had thrown a few more fastballs, Finn asked, "Do you have any other pitches than a fastball?"

"Coach said not to mess around with a curveball yet."

"How old are you?" Finn asked.

"Thirteen. I'll be fourteen in June."

Finn nodded. "Good advice. You don't want hurt your arm. Better to wait a while to start the curveball. How about a changeup?"

Danny lifted up his catcher's mask. "Changeup?" he exclaimed. "He throws nothing but heat. Did he tell you that he threw seventy-five at the fair?"

"Yeah, he told me," Finn said, a small smile spreading across his lips. He looked back at Jack. "So, no changeup?"

"Nah," Jack said. He squinted into the sun. "I never needed one. I struck out just about everybody with fastballs."

Finn laughed. "The way you throw," he said, "I'll bet you did." He took five long strides away from Jack and toward home plate. "You used to throw from here. You were a lot closer to the batter." Finn turned to Danny behind the plate. "How fast did he throw last year?"

"Not as fast as he does now, but plenty fast."

"I'm sure," said Finn. "But in the Rising Stars League you pitch from 60 feet." Finn walked back and slapped a baseball into

Jack's glove. "You're going to need a changeup. We'll work on that." He motioned with his glove to home plate. "Try a few more."

This guy doesn't care how fast I throw, Jack thought as he threw more pitches. *He doesn't care much about anything. He just stands there.*

"Okay, Jack," Finn said, stepping forward. "Let me show you something."

Jack stopped and crossed his arms across his chest.

"A lot of your pitches are high," Finn started. "That's because—"

"That's my riser," Jack interrupted. "I get a lot of strikeouts with it."

"Bet you get a lot of walks, too," Finn said. "How many walks did you give up in your first game?"

"Uh, I don't know," Jack lied. "Five or six." He knew it was six.

Finn looked shocked. "In three innings?" he said. "That's *way* too many."

Jack said nothing. He toed the dirt with his cleats.

"Don't worry," Finn said. "We'll work on that. Let me show you something." He stepped on to the pitching rubber. "You have to extend your arm more, like you're reaching out to the catcher's mitt," he explained as he went through the pitching motion. "That's how you keep the ball low in the strike zone."

"Yeah, but—" Jack began.

"No buts, just listen," Finn said firmly. "When you pitch the ball low in the strike zone, the batter is forced to hit ground balls. And most ground balls turn into easy outs."

"Don't I want to strike people out?" Jack asked.

"You want easy outs," Finn said. "I mean, strikeouts are great. But if you can get the batter to hit ground balls instead of line drives, your fielders can do their jobs. Most of all, you want to put the ball over the plate so the other team has to swing. If they hit the ball, your fielders can make the easy outs."

Jack didn't say anything. But secretly he thought that Finn was a little crazy not to want him to strike out as many batters as he could.

"Now, let me show you the changeup," Finn said. He grabbed a ball from the bucket. "There are a couple of different changeup grips," he went on. "This is the grip for the circle change." He made a circle with the thumb and pointer finger of his left hand, holding the ball with the other three fingers.

"Go ahead," he instructed Jack. "Your hand should be big enough."

Jack placed his fingers on the ball the same way Finn had. "It feels kind of weird," he said, moving his fingers around the ball.

"Yeah, it'll feel funny for a while, but you'll get used to it," Finn said. "Ever heard of Tom Glavine? He threw a circle change."

"I've heard of him. He was a lefty. Played for Atlanta," Jack said. "How fast did he throw?"

"Will you just forget about speed?" Finn sounded a bit annoyed. "Glavine won more than 300 games in the major leagues. That's how fast he threw."

"Okay," Jack said, taking a half step back. "I was just asking."

"Let's see you throw a few to Danny," Finn said. "Just use the same motion as your fastball."

Jack threw several changeups, just as he was told.

After a few pitches Finn nodded. "Pretty good," he said. "You got some nice movement on it. You should be able to throw it over the plate."

"I can't throw it very fast this way," Jack said.

"That's the point," Finn explained. "The batter is expecting your fastball—and then he swings too soon." He glanced to his left. "Hey, look who's here," he said, grinning.

Sarah and Mr. Lerner were walking across the field with the dog. Strikeout saw Finn and started pulling on his leash, making Sarah walk faster. When they reached Finn, Strikeout began wiggling and jumping. Finn laughed and gave Strikeout a couple of quick pats.

"I think he likes you," Sarah said as she

slipped her hand into Finn's.

"So how does Jack look?" Mr. Lerner asked when he caught up with everybody.

"Good." Finn gave Sarah a quick smile, then turned his attention to Mr. Lerner. "He's got a terrific arm and a pretty good motion. There are a few things we have to practice. But he should be a real good pitcher...if he works at it."

Jack shot a glance at Danny and they both rolled their eyes.

"So are you going to take my little brother on as a new student?" Sarah asked. "We could come out and visit on Sundays."

"Sure," Finn agreed. "When Westminster doesn't have a game. We sometimes have to play makeup games on Sundays."

"So what do you say, Jack?" his father asked.

Jack felt trapped. He wasn't so sure about Finn and his ideas about pitching. The guy didn't seem to care how hard Jack threw the ball. He didn't even care if Jack struck anybody out. Letting the batters hit the ball? How crazy was that?

But Sarah sure seemed to like him. And their mom and dad were all excited. Even Strikeout loved Finn.

"Um, sure," Jack said. "Great."

Jack and Danny drifted slowly through the noisy corridors of Landon Middle School, dodging the crowds of kids talking and slamming lockers.

Annie fell into step beside them. "Are you guys coming to our softball game today?"

"What time?" Jack asked.

"Three thirty."

"You pitching?"

"Yeah, of course."

"We'll be there," Jack answered.

"Are *you* pitching tomorrow?" Annie asked Jack.

"Yeah," Jack nodded. "You coming?"

"I'm keeping the scorebook," Annie said. "Remember?" She turned down a corridor. "See you later," she called with a wave.

Jack and Danny kept walking through the crowd.

"Hey, Jack!" Jaylin called from behind them. He waited until Jack turned around. "Did you see that Mr. Pemberton posted the pairings for the Ping-Pong tournament outside his classroom?"

Jack and Danny glanced at the clock outside the principal's office and then at each other. They were thinking the same thing. "If we hurry," Jack said, "we can check out the pairings and be back at the library in time for our Research Methods class."

The boys jogged down the corridor and ran up a flight of stairs.

"No running," warned a teacher near the top of the stairs.

They slowed to a fast walk. Mr. Pemberton, a short man with dark hair and glasses that made him look like an owl, was standing outside his classroom as students scurried past him.

"Hey, Mr. Pemberton," Jack said. "We're here to check out the tournament pairings."

The teacher pointed to a large chart behind him. "They're right here."

Jack and Danny gazed up at the chart and studied the pairings for the school Ping-Pong tournament.

Bye	Jack Lerner
Bye	
Emma Piazza	
Taylor Drayne	
Elena Banks	
Casey Decamp	
Jared Kaplan	
Jeff Badillo	
Pam Lingel	
Connor Howse	
Frankie Lopez	
Charlie Anderson	
Danny Cruz	
Asher Minkoff	
Annie Li	
Clement Williams	
Eleanor Donahue	
Ryan Finn	
Andy Wong	
Jordan Johnson	
Nate Bailey	
Janet Reber	
Elizabeth Evans	
Peter Parker	
Jackson Byrne	
Carol Woodside	
Jared Hillman	
Roy Hargrove	
Ann Voss	
Matt Collogan	
Bye	Eli Roth
Bye	

"I gave you and Eli Roth a bye in the first round, Jack," Mr. Pemberton explained, "because you guys were in the finals last year. And this year we only had thirty kids sign up instead of thirty-two."

"Hey, you're scaring away the competition," Danny teased Jack, poking him playfully in the shoulder. "You and your killer forehand smash."

"We have some new names up there," Mr. Pemberton observed.

"When are the matches?" Jack asked.

"We'll play the first three rounds this Thursday after school," Mr. Pemberton said. "And the semifinals and finals on the next Thursday."

Jack looked down the list of names. "Who's Andy Wong?"

"He's a new kid in my math class," Danny said. "Kind of quiet."

Jack pointed at the brackets. "Poor guy. Eli will probably crush him."

"And you'll crush Eli," Danny said.

"You'd better hurry, guys," Mr. Pemberton said, tapping his wristwatch. "You two have exactly sixty seconds to get to class."

Jack and Danny sped back through the corridor, sprinted down the stairs, and skidded into the library with just a second to spare.

"Nice of you to join us, Mr. Lerner and Mr. Cruz," Mrs. Meredith said from the front of the room. "You can share a computer for your research." She turned to the rest of the class. "Remember, you'll need to cite at least four sources in your papers."

Jack and Danny sat down at a computer in the corner and logged on. "I'm going to look up that guy, Finn," Jack whispered.

"You mean on Facebook?" Danny asked.

Jack shook his head. "No. I want to see what his pitching stats were in college."

"Well, make it quick," Danny advised. "We've got to do some research on Franklin Roosevelt."

Jack was already on the Macalester College website. He pulled up the baseball page.

"When did he graduate?" Danny asked.

"Last year, I think," Jack said. "Or maybe the year before."

"Click on 'Statistics,'" Danny suggested, pointing to the top of the screen.

"Here he is," Jack said.

Year	W-L	IP	H	R	ER	BB	SO	ERA
Fr.	0-0	3.1	8	11	11	3	2	29.70
So.	4-3	58	72	32	27	26	49	4.19
Jr.	3-6	83	82	54	48	28	56	5.20
Sr.	6-4	81	57	36	33	21	61	3.66

Jack almost laughed out loud. "Man, he really stunk his freshman year," he said, studying the rows of numbers. "He only pitched 3.1 innings and had a 29.70 earned run average."

"Yeah, but it looks like he was pretty good after that," Danny observed.

Jack shrugged. "His record for his college career was only thirteen wins and thirteen losses," he said. "That's not so hot."

"It's not bad, either," Danny said, motioning toward the screen. "His team lost most of its games. And look, he struck out a lot of people and only walked a few."

Jack was still unconvinced. "Whatever," he said.

"Heads up," Danny muttered. "Mrs. Meredith's coming."

Jack quickly clicked back to the Macalester home page.

"Now why are you boys on this website?" Mrs. Meredith asked, frowning.

"Um, my sister's boyfriend went to Macalester," Jack said. "And he said his favorite history professor wrote a book on Franklin Roosevelt. I thought we might contact her."

"Really?" Mrs. Meredith said with a funny smile. Then she added, "Get to work, boys."

"I don't think she believed you, Jack," Danny said as Mrs. Meredith moved on.

Jack laughed. "Yeah, I don't either," he said. "But I found out what I wanted to know about Finn."

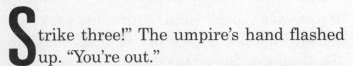

"Strike three!" The umpire's hand flashed up. "You're out."

Coach Bentley popped up from the bench, clapping and shouting. "Good work, Jack. Keep throwing strikes. Go right after them."

Danny took the ball from his mitt and fired it to the third baseman, who tossed it around the horn to the second baseman, who relayed it to the first baseman, who then tossed it to the shortstop.

Jack stepped off the mound and smiled. *Two strikeouts to start the game,* he thought. *All right. Now I'm really throwing.*

The next batter stepped to the plate and Jack got into position. Jack wound up and threw a fastball that sliced the outside corner. The batter never took his bat off his shoulder.

Strike!

The next fastball cut right down the middle of the plate. But the batter couldn't catch up with it.

Strike two!

Jack stood on the mound, moving his fingers over the ball and wondering whether this might be a good time to try the changeup that Finn had shown him.

No, he decided. *I'm gonna blow another fastball right by this batter.* Jack reared back and fired.

Strike three!

The Bears exploded in cheers as they ran in from the field.

"All right, Jack, quick inning!"

"Way to throw!"

Jack grabbed a seat next to Annie. "So, how many pitches did I throw that inning?" he asked with a satisfied smile.

Annie didn't even have to look at the scorebook. "Eleven," she said.

"A little better than last time," he said.

"That's for sure," Annie replied.

Danny plopped down on the bench next to Jack. "Man, you are pitching the lights out today," he said as he unbuckled his chest protector. "Guess that lesson from Finn must have really paid off."

Jack shook his head firmly. "It wasn't the lesson. He didn't teach me anything." He took a long swig of water and stared at the field. The Bears had runners on first and second. "I'm just back in the groove," he said, flashing his friends a grin. "I'm focused."

Jaylin hit a two-run double. The Bears led 2–0 when Jack walked back to the mound at the top of the second inning.

Jack got the first batter to fly out, but only after three balls and two strikes. The second batter topped a weak roller to shortstop. Jaylin charged for it and threw to first base.

Two outs.

The Bears infield filled with chatter.

"One-two-three inning."

"Keep throwing strikes, Jack!"

"No hitter, no hitter."

Jack blazed two fastballs by the batter. No balls, two strikes. One more pitch and he was out of the inning. He thought about throwing the changeup, but decided against it again. He wound up and threw a belt-high fastball across the heart of the plate.

Crack! The batter smacked a line drive over the second baseman's head for a clean single. Jack couldn't believe it!

The center fielder threw in the ball. Jack slapped it angrily into his glove and tugged his cap down as he went into the stretch to face the next batter. His first two pitches sailed high and wide. Two balls, no strikes.

"Settle down now," Coach Bentley called from behind the high chain-link screen. "Throw strikes!"

Jack blistered the next pitch just off the outside corner. The batter started to swing but held back.

"Ball!" the umpire shouted. "Three balls, no strikes."

Jack winced as if he had stepped on a sharp rock. *I needed that strike,* he thought.

The next pitch wasn't close at all. It was way outside.

Ball four.

There were runners at first and second, two outs. Coach Bentley was up and shouting again. "Hang in there, Jack. Bottom of the order."

Jack's eyes narrowed as he focused on Danny's mitt. *Concentrate!* he told himself.

The next pitch was right over the plate, but the batter surprised everyone by laying down a perfect bunt and dashing to first base. Suddenly, after five straight outs, Jack was in big trouble. The bases were loaded with two outs.

Danny called time-out, pushed up his mask, and walked out to talk to Jack. "Come on," he said. "This guy is their ninth batter. He's no hitter. Just throw it right by him. Nothing but strikes."

Jack nodded and Danny got back into position.

Jack took a deep breath and blew out a rush of air. Three of his pitches sailed wide. Two were right over the plate, making the count three balls, two strikes. The bases were loaded with two outs. Jack gripped the ball so hard that his left hand ached. He wound up and fired his hardest fastball.

High. Ball four.

Jack kicked the dirt as each runner moved up a base. The Bears' lead was now just 2–1. The next batter cracked a single up the middle and two more runs scored. The Bears were behind now, 3–2.

Jack's chin sank to his chest. *It seems like I'm throwing heat,* he thought, *and I've still given up three runs.* He took another deep breath, refocused, and got the next batter to pop up for an easy out.

The Bears grabbed the lead again, 4–3, when Danny knocked in two runs with a double in the bottom of the second inning. But in the top of the third, Jack gave up two walks, a hit, and another run. The score was tied when he left the mound and Coach Bentley took him out of the game.

"You pitched better this game," the coach said. "You just had some tough luck."

Annie came over and showed Jack the scorebook.

INNING	PITCHES	STRIKES	BALLS	RUNS
1st	⊮⊮⊮I ⑪	⊮ IIII ⑨	II ②	0
2nd	⊮⊮⊮⊮⊮⊮ ㉘	⊮⊮III ⑬	⊮⊮⊮⊮ ⑮	3
3rd	⊮⊮⊮⊮II ㉒	⊮⊮ ⑩	⊮⊮II ⑫	1
Totals	61	32	29	4

"You were pitching great for a while," she said, pointing to the ball and strike totals.

Jack put on his jacket and took a seat on the bench. He pulled a baseball from his pocket and slowly began trying out a changeup grip. He made a circle with his thumb and pointer and grabbed the ball with his other three fingers—exactly the way Finn had taught him.

Later in the game, with the Bears leading 13–8 in the last inning, Danny joined Jack on the bench. "You were throwing great today," he said. "At least 75 miles per hour. If you'd had a couple of breaks, you would have shut them out."

Jack could only manage a weak smile.

Danny slapped him on the knee. "At least we won," he said. "Don't worry about it. Right now you can just think about winning the Ping-Pong tournament."

Chapter 7

Jack walked into the gym after school with his two favorite paddles tucked under his arm. Looking around, he saw the four Ping-Pong tables set up for the tournament. The matches had already begun and the familiar *plick-plock* of the plastic balls bouncing back and forth filled the air.

A student scorekeeper sat in a chair near each table. Other kids sat in the bleachers, watching the matches and cheering. Jack found Danny in the front row watching Annie compete.

"Hey, here's the champ," Danny said.

"How's it going?" Jack asked, nodding toward the nearby table as he sat down.

"Annie won the first set, 21–14," Danny

said. "And she's leading in the second set. She should beat this guy."

"Yeah. It only takes two sets to win the match." Jack eyed the other tables. "Maybe I should check out the other matches to see who I might be playing in the second round."

Danny shook his head. "Don't even bother," he said. "I saw them. You've got nothing to worry about. They won't even touch your forehand smash."

"Where are you playing?" Jack asked Danny.

"Right here, after Annie."

Jack looked up in time to see Annie smack a low forehand. It bounced deep and flew by the other player for a point. "Nice shot, Annie!" Jack called out. Then he leaned over to Danny. "Have you seen anybody who's any good?"

"Not really."

"What about that new kid, Andy Wong?"

Danny didn't look impressed. "I saw him play a couple of points," he said. "No big deal. All he does is hit it back over the net."

Annie spun a serve low and clean. Her

opponent went for a hard backhand, but the ball caught the net and bounced back. The match ended. Annie shook hands with the player she'd just defeated and walked over to the boys. "Your table, Danny," she said cheerfully. Then she looked at Jack. "When do you play?"

"I'm not sure," Jack said, standing up. "Guess I'd better find Mr. Pemberton."

The history teacher was walking through the gym with a clipboard. "There you are," he said when he saw Jack. "I thought the defending champion had forgotten to show up." He checked the clipboard. "You'll be playing at Table 2 when that match finishes."

"Who am I up against?" Jack asked.

Mr. Pemberton checked the clipboard again. "Taylor Drayne," he said. "He beat Emma Piazza in the first round, 21–17 and 21–16."

* * *

Jack bounced on the balls of his feet at Table 2, getting ready for his first match.

The scorekeeper set her stopwatch. "You guys have three minutes to warm up," she said.

Jack felt confident as the ball bounced back and forth. Danny had been right. This opponent would be easy to beat. Jack decided he could use the match to practice some of his riskier shots.

"Okay. Time to start the match," the score-keeper announced.

Jack kept the points and rallies going so he could get a feel for his shots. But when one of Taylor's returns bounced high, Jack smashed back a forehand so hard that Taylor didn't even try to hit it.

Danny and Annie cheered from the stands.

"What a shot!"

"Point, Lerner."

Jack's forehand smash was like his best fastball last year. No one could touch it. He won his first match with ease, 21–3 and 21–5, and then hustled over to watch Danny and Annie play each other.

As he watched his friends, Jack kept an

eye on Andy Wong at Table 3. Andy looked quick and confident, moving easily from side to side. He never went for a big smash. Instead, he seemed content to guide the ball back over the net and wait for his opponent to send a shot long or hit one into the net.

Eli will probably beat him, Jack thought. *This new guy doesn't hit very hard.*

"Hey, Jack," Mr. Pemberton called from across the gym. "Get ready for your next match. You're at Table 2 again."

Jack's second opponent, Elena Banks, was tougher than Taylor. She had a tricky serve and a variety of spin shots that gave Jack some trouble at first. But after a few points Jack got his forehand smash going again and pulled away to win in straight sets, 21–13 and 21–7.

At the end of the day, Jack, Danny, and Annie checked the brackets posted on the gym wall.

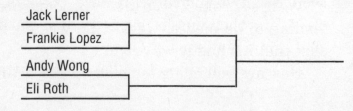

"Looks like it'll be you against Eli in the finals again," Danny said.

Annie pointed at the brackets. "Frankie Lopez is pretty good," she said. "He'll give you a tough match."

Danny shrugged. "He's not *that* good."

"What do you know?" Jack teased. "You lost in the second round," he said, pointing to Annie. "To her!"

"Hey, what's that supposed to mean?" Annie said, pretending to be insulted.

"I'm just kidding." Then Jack got serious. "What about the new guy?" he asked. "Do you think he can beat Eli? Wong's pretty laid back, but he was racking up the points over there."

Both Jack's friends shook their heads. "Nah," Annie said. "He just kind of floats the ball back over the net."

"I bet you'll still be the champ this time next week," Danny said Jack.

"We'll see," Jack said. He was only pretending to be modest. Inside, he was confident that his buddy was right.

"Hey, are you going to catch for me again

Sunday?" Jack asked Danny. "That guy Finn's coming over again."

"Can't," Danny said. "It's my granddad's eightieth birthday."

"I'll do it," Annie volunteered.

"Okay, thanks," Jack said. "Be at the field around two thirty, okay?"

"What's Finn like?" Annie asked.

"My sister likes him," Jack said as he turned to walk out of the gym. "But I don't think he's so great."

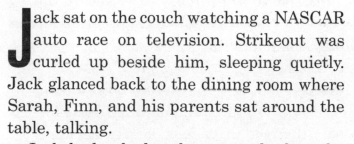

Chapter 8

J ack sat on the couch watching a NASCAR
auto race on television. Strikeout was
curled up beside him, sleeping quietly.
Jack glanced back to the dining room where
Sarah, Finn, and his parents sat around the
table, talking.

Jack had asked to be excused when the
conversation turned to books. *For a baseball
guy, Finn sure reads a lot,* Jack thought. He
checked his phone for the time: 2:20. He
wondered if Finn had forgotten about their
lesson. *Maybe I should call Annie and tell
her we'll be late.*

"You a big NASCAR fan?" Finn asked.

Jack almost dropped his phone. He hadn't
heard Finn come into the living room. "Not

really," Jack said, getting to his feet. "It's the only thing on besides golf."

"Isn't there a baseball game on ESPN?" Finn asked.

"Probably. But my mom and dad won't let us get cable." Jack glanced back at the race, where the cars roared around the track just inches from each other's bumpers.

"I hear you." Finn gestured toward the TV screen. "I saw a show once where a driver explained how you win a race."

Jack laughed. "That's easy," he said. "You drive as fast as you can and don't crash."

"Nope," Finn said, shaking his head. "He said that you drive as *slow* as you can."

"Huh?" *This guy's crazy,* Jack thought.

"Yeah, you drive as slow as you can," Finn repeated. "And still win the race." He slapped Jack on the shoulder. "Hey, grab your glove. I'll go change into my sweats."

* * *

When Jack and Finn reached the field, Annie was already there throwing softballs, under-hand, into the backstop.

54

Jack made the introductions. "This is Annie," he told Finn. "She's a pitcher, too."

"I don't know how to throw underhand," Finn said with a grin, "so I probably can't help you." He pointed to the backstop. "Let's see you throw a couple more."

Annie zipped a pitch that clanged against the backstop.

"What were you aiming for?" Finn asked.

"Nothing, really," Annie replied.

"Always aim at something," Finn said. "At least I know that much." He turned to Jack. "Okay, let's get going. You're catching, right, Annie?"

"Yeah."

"Got a mask?"

Annie held up a catcher's mask. "It's Danny's," she said, pulling it down over her face.

"Good. Give Jack a good low target over the outside corner of the plate," Finn told her. He plunked down a bucket of baseballs behind the pitcher's mound. Then he looked back at Jack. "Did you work on the changeup I showed you last time?"

"A little." Jack shrugged. "Not much." He

could almost feel Finn rolling his eyes behind his sunglasses.

"Let's start with a few fastballs," Finn suggested, tossing a baseball to Jack.

Finally, he's making sense, Jack thought. He went into his windup and fired hard. The ball sailed high and wide. Annie reached up and snapped it out of the air. Each of Jack's first few pitches were the same: fast, but out of the strike zone.

Finn flipped another ball to Jack. "Let's try mixing in a strike every once in a while," he said coolly.

Jack bit his lip and said nothing. He would show this guy with his next pitch. Then he wound up and fired his hardest fastball.

Smack! Annie didn't move her mitt.

Jack tried to keep from smiling.

"Nice pitch," Finn said, nodding. "Let's see you do it again."

This guy's brutal, Jack thought. He wound up and threw hard again, but the ball flew wide and high.

Finn stepped forward. "Remember what I

showed you last week?" he asked. He went through the pitching motion again, step by step. "Reach out more toward your target. Stay on top of it. That'll keep the ball low." He pointed toward home plate. "Remember, you want to keep the ball low and away, not in the middle of the plate. Anybody can hit the ball if it's right down the middle...no matter how fast you throw it."

Finn handed Jack another ball and stepped back. "What I'm telling you may feel funny at first," he said. "But if you keep practicing it, you'll control your fastball much better. And if you can control your fastball, you'll cut down on your walks and get more outs."

Jack threw a few more pitches, only half-trying to do what Finn had told him.

Finally, Finn held onto the ball. "Are you okay?" he asked Jack. "I mean...is something wrong?"

Jack stepped off the mound and away from Finn. "I don't know," he said. "Whenever I do what you say, I don't throw it as fast."

Finn took a deep breath. "Is that all you think pitching is?" he asked impatiently. "Throwing the ball fast?"

"Are you guys going to throw any more?" Annie asked from home plate.

"I don't know," Finn said. "It depends. Are we, Jack?"

For a while Jack didn't answer. Then he blurted out, "I looked you up, you know."

"What are you talking about?" Finn asked.

"I checked out your pitching record on the Macalester College website," Jack said. "You weren't that great. You only had a 13–13 record."

"I did all right," Finn said. "I'm proud I got the most I could out of my ability." Then he looked straight at Jack. "You seem to be real impressed with guys who throw the ball fast," he said. "Do you know who threw the hardest in the history of baseball?"

"I don't know. Randy Johnson?" Jack guessed. "Roger Clemens?"

"They threw hard," Finn said. "But the guy I'm talking about threw 105 miles per hour."

Jack's head snapped back. "Really? Who?"

"Steve Dalkowski."

"Never heard of him," Jack said.

"That's my point," Finn said. "He threw hard, but he never made it out of the minors because he couldn't throw strikes." He gave the baseball a little toss. "So, ever heard of Sandy Koufax?"

"Sure," Jack answered. "Koufax pitched for the Dodgers. He was a Hall of Famer. *He* threw really hard."

"Yeah," Finn agreed. "But the thing is, he didn't become great until he stopped walking batters."

Jack frowned. It seemed like Finn didn't even care about throwing hard.

"Listen, if you want to get better, I think I can help you," Finn went on. "But if you just want to keep throwing instead of pitching..." His voice trailed off.

Jack didn't know what to say. *Better?* he thought. *How can Finn help me get better? He only threw 80 miles an hour in college.*

"When do you pitch next?" Finn asked.

"Tuesday."

Finn pulled his wallet out of his sweat-pants pocket. "Here's my card," he said.

"Send me an e-mail after Tuesday's game and tell me how you did," he suggested. "And let me know if you'd like to try another practice session, okay?"

Jack looked at the card and then at Finn. *Why does Sarah like this guy?* he wondered. *He's such a know-it-all.*

"Okay," Jack said, taking Finn's card. But he wasn't sure he wanted any more lessons.

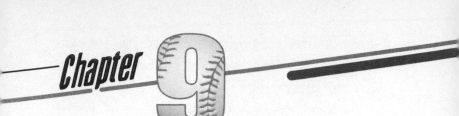

Chapter 9

"How am I doing?" Jack asked as he sat down on the bench. Annie pointed to the scoreboard beyond the center field fence. "You're ahead 3–1 after four innings," she said. "That's how you're doing."

"No, you know what I mean," Jack said, trying to sneak a peek at the scorebook. "How many pitches so far?"

Annie checked the book. Jack could see her lips moving as she counted up the pitches. "Sixty-one," she said. "You had thirty-nine strikes, twenty-two balls. Only one walk."

"Do you think Coach Bentley will leave me in?" Jack asked.

Annie looked around the field. "Well, he doesn't have anyone warming up," she observed. "He'll probably keep you in for one more inning." Her face brightened. "Maybe you'll get the win."

"We need every win we can get if we're going to make the playoffs," Jack said, punching the pocket of his baseball glove.

The Bears went down in order, one-two-three. Coach Bentley walked in from coaching third base. "Okay, Jack, you're back on the mound," he said. "Keep throwing strikes."

Jack popped off the bench and hustled to the mound. He still felt good after four innings. But the fifth inning quickly turned into a struggle. Jack walked the leadoff batter after letting the count go to three balls, two strikes. He took a deep breath as the batter jogged to first base. *Settle down,* he told himself. *Just throw strikes.*

The first pitch to the second batter whistled across the outside corner for strike one. But the next four pitches were wide of the mark. Another walk. Another base-runner. Now there were runners at first and second with no outs.

"Time," the coach called and slowly walked to the mound.

"Take it easy," he said to Jack. "We still have a 3–1 lead. Just put the ball over the plate." Coach Bentley looked around at the infielders who had crowded in close to them. "Let's try to get a force-out at one of the bases."

The next batter slapped a grounder to Jaylin. The Bears shortstop flipped the ball to the second baseman, who touched the bag for the force-out. Jack let out a deep breath, but he couldn't relax. Runners at first and third, one out.

As Jack delivered the next pitch, the runner at first took off for second base.

Ball one. Danny sprang to his feet and faked a throw to second. The runner on third fell for the fake and started toward home. Danny quickly turned and fired the ball to third. The runner scrambled and dove back to the base.

Safe!

"Time!" Danny called and walked out to Jack. "I didn't want to throw to second because of the guy at third," he said. "Anyway, I figure you're gonna strike out the next two batters."

Danny was right about the first batter. Jack whipped three fastballs past him for the second out.

The Bears infield filled with hope and chatter.

"Come on, Jack, one more out."

"Two outs. Just throw strikes."

"Let's make a play for him."

Jack fell behind the next batter with two high pitches.

"Come on, Jack, no free passes!" Danny yelled from his crouched position. "Let's get this guy!" He set his mitt along the outside corner, just like he'd done when Jack had practiced his pitching with Finn.

Jack wound up and threw hard. His fastball drifted away from Danny's target and over the middle of the plate.

Crack! The batter smacked a hard line drive to center field. Ben, the Bears center fielder, ran and dove, stretching his glove toward the sinking liner. The ball lodged in the webbing of Ben's glove, but came loose when he hit the ground. The runners at second and third sprinted home. The score was tied 3–3.

Coach Bentley walked slowly out to the mound. "Sorry, Jack, I'm taking you out," he said, as Jack handed him the baseball. "You've thrown a lot of pitches."

Jack touched gloves and bumped fists with his teammates as he made his way to the end of the Bears bench.

"Good effort."

"Way to throw."

"Great job."

But Jack knew that wasn't true. He sat on the bench, thinking: *Same old story. Too many walks.*

* * *

Jack was still in his uniform and thinking about the game when he walked through his front door. Strikeout ran up to him, wagging his tail.

"Hey, Jack. How'd it go today?" his mother

asked, looking up from her laptop. His father was across the room, working on his own laptop.

"Okay," Jack said. "We won 5–4."

"How'd you do?" his father asked.

Jack stopped near the foot of the stairs, feeling tired and dirty. He really needed a hot shower. "All right, I guess. I pitched almost five innings and gave up three runs."

His father nodded. "Sounds pretty good."

"It sounds *very* good," his mother said. "I think Finn must be helping you a lot, Jack."

"Maybe. I'm going take a shower." Jack started up the stairs. Then, feeling a grumble in his stomach, he added, "When are we going to eat?"

"We're planning to pick up some Chinese food," his father said. "Is that okay?"

"Sure. Put me down for some sweet-and-sour chicken."

Jack ran upstairs. He sat down at his computer, still in his dirty uniform, and logged on to www.baseball-reference.com. He typed "Steve Dalkowski" into the search box. Rows of numbers appeared on the screen.

Year	W-L	IP	H	R	ER	BB	SO	ERA
1957	1-8	62	22	68	56	129	121	8.13
1958	4-10	118	53	110	100	245	232	7.63
1959	4-7	84	41	81	73	190	142	7.82
1960	7-15	170	105	120	97	262	262	5.14
1961	3-12	103	75	117	96	196	150	8.39
1962	7-10	160	117	61	54	114	192	3.04
1963	2-4	41	27	18	17	40	36	3.73
1964	10-6	135	126	63	55	92	166	3.67
1965	8-8	122	119	85	68	86	95	5.02
Total	46-80	995	682	723	616	1354	1396	5.59

W-L – Win/Loss record
IP – Innings pitched
H – Hits
R – Runs

ER – Earned runs
BB – Bases on balls (walks)
SO – Strikeouts
ERA – Earned Run Average

Hmmm, they're all minor league stats, Jack told himself. *Finn was right. This guy never made it to the majors.* He studied the screen. "Let's look up Koufax," he muttered as he typed.

More numbers popped up on the screen.

Year	W-L	IP	H	R	ER	BB	SO	ERA
1955	2-2	41.2	33	15	14	28	30	3.02
1956	2-4	58.2	66	37	32	29	30	4.91
1957	5-4	104.1	83	49	45	51	122	3.88
1958	11-11	158.2	132	89	79	105	131	4.48
1959	8-6	153.1	136	74	69	92	173	4.05
1960	8-13	175	133	83	76	100	197	3.91
1961	18-13	255.2	212	117	100	96	269	3.52
1962	14-7	184.1	134	61	52	57	216	2.54
1963	25-5	311	214	68	65	58	306	1.88
1964	19-5	223	154	49	43	53	223	1.74
1965	26-8	335.2	216	90	76	71	382	2.04
1966	27-9	323	241	74	62	77	317	1.73

Jack's eyes went straight to the "BB" column for bases on balls, or walks.

Looks like Finn was right again, Jack thought. *Koufax got a lot better around 1961 and 1962, after he stopped walking so many batters.*

Jack pulled his sweaty uniform shirt over his head and tossed it in a heap in the corner of his room. He sat back in his chair and stared at the screen. Maybe Finn knew something about pitching after all.

Chapter 10

Jack heard the noise from the Landon gym before he and his friends reached the door. The bleachers were packed with students and teachers talking and laughing. This Thursday afternoon, there was only one Ping-Pong table set up. And it was right in the center.

"I didn't think there would be so many people here," Annie said.

"Guess they want to see the champ here defend his title," Danny said, nudging Jack.

"Or they want to see me lose it," Jack said.

Mr. Pemberton walked briskly over to them. "You have the second semifinal match, Jack," he said. "Eli and Andy will play the first match."

"Good," Danny whispered. "We'll be able to scout them."

Jack nodded.

The three friends squeezed into the front row of the bleachers. Jack watched closely as the players warmed up. Andy was quick and athletic. His strokes had no wasted motion. He didn't try to smash the ball over the net. Instead, he seemed happy to spin it back with a short jab of a stroke.

Jack was amazed at how consistent Andy was—the guy almost never missed a shot. Like a pitcher who only threw strikes or a basketball point guard who never lost his dribble, Andy kept sending the ball back over the net, even from the most difficult angles.

As the first semifinal match began, Eli jumped to an early 9–6 lead. But he couldn't match Andy's consistency. Eli began to make mistakes, spinning a forehand into the net or sailing a backhand long. Andy slowly began to come back, then went ahead. He won the first set, 21–17.

"Don't worry," Danny said. "Eli doesn't have your super smash."

"I don't know," Annie said, her forehead knitted in concern. "Andy looks really good. He's kind of boring to watch, but it's like he never misses."

"Maybe Eli can come back and beat him," Jack said, almost hoping. *I've played Eli before. I know I can beat him,* he thought.

But Eli didn't come back. In the second set, Andy grabbed the lead and never let it go. He won the second set and the match, 21–15.

"Good game," Eli said, as the two boys shook hands.

"Thanks," said Andy with a nod. "Good game."

Eli took a towel from the scorekeeper and grabbed a seat next to Jack.

"Too bad," Jack said. "You played great."

"Wong's tougher than he looks," Eli said, wiping his face. "Good luck."

Jack didn't need much luck in his semifinal match. He won the first set, 21–12. The second set was closer, 21–16, but Jack never felt worried, even for a moment, that he might lose.

"The final championship match between Jack Lerner and Andy Wong will begin in five minutes," Mr. Pemberton announced to the crowd.

The gym began buzzing with talk about the big match. Danny's voice rose above the noise of the crowd. "Andy's never seen a smash like Jack's," he told anyone who would listen. "It's not even gonna be close."

At first it looked as if Danny's prediction would be right.

Jack whipped a couple of smashes by Andy and grabbed an early 10–5 lead. But after a while Andy seemed to adjust to the speed of Jack's forehand smash. He played a little farther from the table, floating the ball back return after return no matter how hard Jack hit it.

Slowly, steadily, Andy worked his way back to tie the match 17–17. Jack spun a serve to begin a crucial point. The ball flew back and forth across the net dozens of times, darting and spinning at new and sharper angles. The kids in the bleachers cheered louder and louder with each shot.

This guy never misses, Jack thought as he smacked another forehand across the net.

Finally, one of Andy's returns bounced high. Jack saw his chance. He leaped forward and whacked a forehand with all his might. But the ball spun a hair too low, caught the top ribbon of the net, and fell back on Jack's side. Andy's point. For the first time in the match, Jack was behind, 18–17.

Suddenly, Jack felt his confidence crumbling. It was like when he was on the mound with bases loaded, struggling to throw strikes. A couple of careless points later, he lost the first set, 21–18.

Still shaken, Jack fell behind early in the second set. He battled back and had a chance to tie the score at 15–all, but smashed a forehand too hard. It missed the table by an inch.

Jack took a deep breath. *Now I'm in trouble,* he thought. *I'm down 16–14 and it's his serve.*

The kids in the crowd were pounding their feet and cheering wildly.

"Come on, Jack, hang in there!"

"Serve it out, Andy. You got him!"

"Let's go, Jack. It's comeback time!"

Mr. Pemberton held up his hands. "Quiet," he ordered loudly. Then he lowered his voice. "Your serve, Andy."

Andy skipped a couple of serves low and hard. Jack went for a big return but spun them long.

"18–14," Mr. Pemberton called out.

Jack bounced on his toes, trying to get some energy back into his legs. He won the next point by angling a sharp backhand.

"18–15," Mr. Pemberton called as Jack pumped his fist.

The next point seemed to go on forever. Jack hit smash after smash, but Andy returned every one, floating them back over the net. Then one of Andy's soft returns clipped the very edge of the table on Jack's side and fell away from Jack's paddle.

"Point," Mr. Pemberton announced. "Andy leads, 19–15."

Jack's heart sank. By now, his legs felt like lead weights. He'd hit hundreds of shots and had very few points to show for it. On the next point, he sent another forehand long and found himself down, 20–15.

"Five straight serves!" Danny yelled from the crowd. "You can do it, champ!"

Jack's serve started another long point, with the ball flying over the net ten... fifteen...twenty times. One of his backhand returns bounced high on Andy's side of the net. But this time, instead of hanging back and hitting a soft return, Andy lunged forward, reached back with his paddle, and smashed a forehand. Jack couldn't react in time. He just stood there—stunned—as the ball slammed against the table and went flying.

"Point, set, and match to Andy Wong," Mr. Pemberton announced. "We have a new champion!" The crowd cheered.

Still in shock, Jack walked to the other side of the table and congratulated Andy. Then he tucked his paddle under his arm and walked out with his friends.

"Hey, he was just lucky," Danny insisted as they pushed through the gym doors. "No way he should've won."

"Then he must've been lucky the whole

match," Annie pointed out. "Did you see that last shot? Wow!"

"Yeah," Jack agreed. "He had that smash shot the whole time. Guess he was saving it for the end." He shook his head. "You're right, Annie. He wasn't lucky. He was just good."

* * *

Jack was glad no one except Strikeout was around when he got home. He didn't feel like telling his mom or dad about the Ping-Pong tournament. He still couldn't believe he'd lost. Grabbing an apple off the kitchen counter, he headed upstairs and logged onto his computer. As he waited for the home page to come up, he spotted Finn's card in the pile of papers on his desk.

He stared at it, thinking about the Ping-Pong finals. Then he thought about Steve Dalkowski, Sandy Koufax, and all the batters he had walked this season. Finally he carefully typed Finn's e-mail address and wrote a short message:

Finn—

Sorry I forgot to write about Tuesday. I went 4.2 innings and gave up 3 runs. I struck out 5 but walked 3. Are you coming Sunday? See you then.

Jack

He had barely hit Send when he got an instant message.

J—

Sounds like you did okay on Tuesday.

See you Sunday.

F

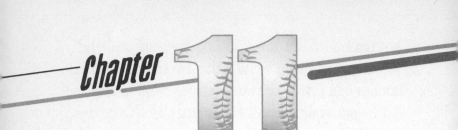

S o what happened in the fifth inning?"
Finn asked. Jack could feel the warm
spring sunshine on his back as he stood
in back of the elementary school. "I don't
know," he said, looking around the field. "I
was throwing pretty well...a lot of strikes. I
don't know...I just walked a couple of guys to
start the inning."

"Walks hurt," Finn said. "Especially to the
leadoff batters in the inning. What part of
the batting order were they?"

Jack shrugged. "I don't remember."

"You've got to know that," Finn said
sternly. "Guys are at the top or the bottom of
the batting order for a reason."

Jack nodded. He didn't need his sister's

boyfriend to explain that coaches put their weaker hitters at the bottom of the batting order.

"So go right after those guys at the bottom of the order," Finn went on. "Did you try the changeup?"

"Not much."

Finn eyed Jack with suspicion. "Have you been practicing it?" he asked.

"I, uh, haven't had a chance," Jack said, trying to think of an excuse. "My friends have been really busy so...I've got nobody to catch me."

Finn was quiet. He pointed to the wall of reddish orange bricks. "How long has this school been here?"

Jack looked at his sister's boyfriend as if he thought he was crazy. "I don't know...a long time. But—"

Finn didn't wait for him to finish. "I mean isn't this brick wall always here?" he said, pointing to the bricks. "You don't need any-body to catch you. You can practice against this wall."

He reached into his equipment bag and

pulled out a piece of hard white rubber shaped like a home plate. Then he walked over to the wall and set down the rubber plate. Taking a piece of yellow chalk from his sweatpants, he chalked up two bricks to mark the lower outside corner of the strike zone.

What is this guy doing? Jack wondered.

He watched as Finn paced twenty steps from the plate, about 60 feet, and motioned to him. "Let's see you throw your fastball from here and hit the chalk on those two bricks," Finn said.

"That's a pretty small area," Jack protested. "The strike zone's a lot bigger than that."

"We're not interested in the whole strike zone," Finn said firmly. "Any good pitcher can throw inside the strike zone. You have to practice hitting the outside corner to get right-handed batters out. And most batters are right-handed."

"Yeah, but—" Jack started.

Finn wasn't listening. He pushed his sunglasses back up on his nose and crossed his arms against his chest. "Go ahead," he said, nodding toward the bricks.

Jack's pitches were high and outside, then low and inside. They seemed to hit everywhere on the wall except the two chalked-up bricks.

"Hold it," Finn said, stepping forward. "Remember what I told you the other day? Extend your arm more, like you're reaching for those bricks. Stay on top of it. That'll keep the ball low." He pointed to home plate. "You want to keep the ball low and away, not in the middle of the plate. That's why I marked those bricks."

"Oh," Jack said. The whole chalk thing made more sense now.

"Like I told you before, anybody can hit the ball if it's right down the middle," Finn said. He grinned. "Even if you throw as fast as Steve Dalkowski."

Jack threw some more pitches. He began to zero in on the two bricks, and several balls smacked against the yellow chalk.

"That's it!" Finn said. "Great job. You're really pitching now."

Jack kept throwing as Finn offered a steady stream of encouragement and advice. "Good. Nice pitch. That's it...that was real close. Remember, stay on top."

After a flurry of fastballs that landed closer to the two bricks, Finn stepped in again. "Okay, that's much better. Now let's work on that changeup."

"I've got to hit those bricks with a changeup?" Jack asked in disbelief.

Finn smiled and shook his head. "No, that's the cool thing about a changeup," he explained. "You just have to throw it across the plate. Remember, this is a slower pitch. So you're just trying to fool the hitter. He'll be expecting your fastball and swing too soon."

He flipped Jack a ball. "Go ahead. Let's see your changeup," he said. "Try to keep it low."

Jack's first attempt was terrible. It bounced five feet in front of the plate. "Maybe not *that* low," Finn said with a grin. Then he checked Jack's grip on the ball and showed him how to release the pitch.

Jack gave it another try. At least the ball hit the wall this time. He kept throwing until he began to feel more comfortable.

The sun was getting warmer and the sweat on Jack's back made his practice shirt stick to his skin. He was working hard, but it felt good.

After a while, his changeups were floating over the plate.

"Okay," Finn said, stepping in one last time. "Nice workout. You're looking much better."

"The changeup feels okay now," Jack agreed, reaching for his water bottle.

"Good. Well, I should get back," Finn said, glancing at his watch. "Your sister will be wondering where I am."

Jack chugged his water as Finn kept talking. "Here's what I want you to do," he said. "Throw forty fastballs and twenty changeups every practice session. But mix it up. Throw two fastballs and then a changeup. And keep track of how many times you hit those two bricks with your fastball."

"Hit them?" Jack asked.

"*Hit* them," Finn repeated. "*Almost* doesn't count."

"But it's only two bricks," Jack protested. "That's pretty tough."

"I know," Finn said. "But pitching is hard and getting better as a pitcher is even harder. Anyway, keep track of how many changeups you throw for strikes, too. Remember, with a changeup, you just have to get it in the strike zone."

"You want me to write everything down?" Jack asked.

"Yeah. Make a chart and record how many fastballs out of the forty hit the bricks and how many changeups are strikes," Finn instructed. "I bet you'll start seeing a big improvement after a couple of workouts."

Jack and Finn started walking back to Jack's house together. The hot day felt a bit like summer.

Jack took off his baseball cap to wipe his sweaty hair away from his face. "How often should I practice?" he asked, lengthening his stride to keep up with Finn.

"What day do you pitch in games?" Finn asked.

"Tuesdays, usually."

"You should play catch every day to build up your arm. But do the pitching practice maybe twice a week. How about Thursday and Saturday?"

Jack nodded.

"And no more excuses about missing a practice session or not having anyone to throw with, okay?" Finn said. "Remember, that brick wall is always there." He eyed Jack. "So what do you say? Deal?"

Jack grinned. "Deal," he answered.

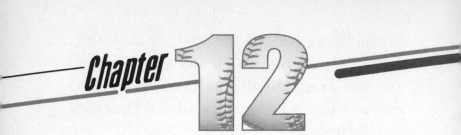

Chapter 12

*T*hump!

The baseball thudded against one of the yellow bricks.

"Two out of seven," Jack muttered to himself. "Not bad." He picked up another ball from the plastic bucket, repeating Finn's instructions in his mind. *Keep the ball low. Reach for the target, then throw. Stay on top of it.* Then he went into his windup.

Thump!

The ball smacked against the wall, missing the two chalked bricks by inches. Jack stood for a moment, staring at the wall. *That was pretty close,* he thought. *The batter would have swung at the pitch. It was really a strike.* He took a deep breath and reached for another baseball. *Three for eight,* he thought. *No. Better not count that last one. It didn't hit the yellow bricks. Two for eight.*

He kept throwing pitches against the brick wall—*thump...thump...thump.* Then he trudged around, picking up the scattered baseballs and putting them back into the plastic bucket.

Not bad, Jack told himself as he plopped the bucket down on the marked spot, 60 feet from the wall. *A few more pitches and I'm done.*

The brim of Jack's baseball cap darkened with a line of sweat. He wound up and threw a changeup that drifted over the plate.

"Hey, what's with the wall?" a voice called. Jack looked up and saw Danny rounding the corner of the school.

"I can't believe it," Danny said as he came up. "You traded me in for a bunch of bricks. I'm not that bad a catcher, am I?"

"Nah. I'm just working on my changeup," Jack said.

"No wonder it's been getting better," Danny said. "You totally fooled that kid from Sanders Corner last week." He imitated a batter swinging for the fences and then looking back in surprise.

Jack laughed. "The changeup wasn't *that* good."

"So come on, I thought we were going to hang out at your house," Danny said.

Jack reached into the bucket for another baseball.

"Hold on, I haven't finished my practice yet," he said. "Finn says I have to throw twenty changeups. That means I have to throw some more."

Danny moved to stand behind Jack. "Okay, I'll call balls and strikes," he said. "Hey, what are those two yellow bricks?"

Jack turned to face his friend. "I practice hitting those with my fastball," he said. "Finn says he wants me to *own* the outside part of the plate."

"Well, you have been spotting your fastball a lot better the last couple of games," Danny agreed.

"I've been practicing," Jack said with a smile.

"Yeah, without me." Danny pretended to be hurt. "Let's see your changeup."

Jack went into his windup and threw.

"Ball!" Danny shouted.

Jack turned around again. "Ball?" he said in disbelief. "That was right over!"

Danny angled his hand against his chest. "It was a little high." He nodded toward the brick wall. "By the way, your new catcher is terrible. He can't catch a thing."

* * *

The boys burst into Jack's house. "I've got to write my scores down before I forget them," Jack said. He tossed his glove and hat on a sofa, waking up Strikeout, who jumped off the cushions and followed the boys to Jack's room, his tail wagging.

Jack sat down at his computer and logged on.

"So how have you been doing?" Danny asked.

Jack pushed his chair back and pointed at the screen. "Take a look," he said.

Date	Fastballs	Change Ups
4/29	5 / 40	6 / 20
5/1	7 / 40	5 / 20
5/6	5 / 40	8 / 20
5/8	9 / 40	10 / 20
5/13	12 / 40	13 / 20
5/15	13 / 40	15 / 20

"Pretty good," Danny said as he studied the chart. "Do you have a chart for the games you've pitched, too?"

"What do you think?" Jack smiled and touched a few keys. Another chart appeared on the screen.

Date	Score	IP	R	H	BB	SO
4/6	L 9-5	3	6	2	6	5
4/13	W 13-8	3	4	4	4	4
4/20	W 5-4	4.2	3	3	3	5
4/27	L 5-2	4	3	3	3	4
5/4	W 6-3	5	2	4	2	3
5/11	W 4-2	5	2	3	1	3
5/18						

Danny pulled closer and studied the chart. He pointed to a line near the middle where Jack's pitching results had improved. "Hey, is this where Finn started giving you pitching lessons?"

"No," Jack answered.

Danny looked surprised.

"That's when I started *listening* to Finn," Jack said with a grin.

"Are you going to be able to keep your streak going on Tuesday?" Danny asked.

"I hope so," Jack answered. "If we win on Tuesday, we'll make it into the playoffs." He opened the Landon Bears baseball schedule on the school's website.

Together the boys studied the ups and downs of the Bear season.

"I didn't think we'd have a chance to make the playoffs at the beginning of the season," Danny said.

"Especially the way I was pitching," Jack admitted.

Danny shrugged. "Yeah, but with the way you're pitching now," he said, "we may *win* the playoffs."

"Maybe," Jack said. "But first we have to make them."

Date	Opponent	Score
4/6	Hornell	L 9-5
4/9	Maury	W 9-4
4/13	Ashburton	W 13-8
4/16	Washington Latin	L 10-5
4/20	Cashell	W 5-4
4/23	Emerick	L 8-3
4/27	Stone Robinson	L 5-2
4/30	Lewistown	W 12-5
5/4	Lafayette	W 6-3
5/7	Damascus	L 7-6
5/11	Sanders Corner	W 4-2
5/14	Lynnfield	W 15-5
5/18	Stafford	
5/21	Playoffs – TBA	

Okay, big game today." Coach Bentley gathered the Bears into a tight huddle. "If we win, we're in the playoffs. If we lose, the season is over."

Jack looked around the group and saw Danny, Jaylin, and the rest of their teammates nodding. Over his shoulder, he saw his mother, father, and Sarah sitting in the stands behind home plate. His mom gave him a thumbs-up. Everyone knew how much this game counted.

"Here's the lineup," Coach Bentley went on. He named the usual starters, then ended with "and Jack is pitching."

The Bears were up first. Jack and Annie grabbed seats on the bench. Jack nervously rubbed his thighs as his knees bounced jumpily in front of him.

"You okay?" Annie asked.

"Yeah," Jack said. "Just a little wound up."

"Don't worry, you'll be fine," Annie assured him. "You've been pitching much better lately." She tapped the scorebook with her pencil. "I know, I've been keeping track. Just keep throwing strikes."

"I'll try," Jack said as he studied the Stafford pitcher. The tall, hard-throwing right-hander whipped three straight fastballs past Jaylin to start the inning.

The Bears shortstop came back to the bench, shaking his head. "You better be good today," he muttered to Jack. "This guy throws fast...real fast."

The Bears went down 1-2-3 in the top of the first and Jack jogged out to the mound for his warm-up tosses. He was still a bit nervous, but went over Finn's familiar instructions in his head as he gazed at the leadoff hitter. *Reach out toward the catcher's mitt. Stay on top of it. That'll keep the ball low. Remember, keep the ball low and away, not in the middle of the plate.*

Jack got into position, wound up, and threw a fastball that just nipped the outside corner.

"Strike one!" the umpire shouted.

The batter fouled off the next pitch for strike two. Jack moved his fingers across the ball for the changeup, exactly the way Finn had taught him. Then he wound up and threw hard. But the ball didn't go very fast. It floated right by the surprised batter for strike three. The infield erupted in cheers.

"All right, Jack!"

"Sweet pitch."

"Good start. Keep it going."

Jack got the second batter on an easy pop fly. But the third batter battled Jack hard, fouling off a couple of good fastballs. With the count two balls and two strikes, Jack switched to his changeup again. The pitch drifted high.

Crack!

The ball flew over Jaylin's head for a clean single. There was a runner on first and two outs with the Stafford cleanup hitter coming to the plate.

All right, settle down, Jack told himself.

Get the next batter. Give your team a chance to win.

Jack shook off Danny's sign for a fastball and started the hitter with a changeup. The Stafford slugger swung hard, but he was too far in front of the pitch. He tapped a weak roller to Jaylin at shortstop, who tossed the ball to first base for the third out.

Jack ran in and sat down next to Annie. Instead of asking her how many pitches he'd thrown, he waited to see what she would say.

"Good inning," Annie said finally. "Not too many pitches."

Danny didn't bother taking off his catching gear. He grabbed a seat next to Jack. "Nice changeup," he said, lifting off his mask and shaking his sweaty hair.

"Thanks," Jack said. "I figured he'd be looking for a fastball and swinging too quick."

The game settled into a tight pitchers' duel. The Bears could only scratch out a pair of singles in the first four innings. Jack worked a couple of quick innings, giving up only one more hit. He didn't strike out any batters, but he kept his fastballs and change-ups low in the strike zone. The Stafford hitters grounded the low pitches to the Bears infielders for easy outs. And Jack didn't give up any walks in the first three innings. He was feeling great as he headed to the mound in the bottom of the fourth.

Coach Bentley jumped to his feet, encouraging his team as they took the field in the bottom of the fourth inning, tied 0–0. "Come on, good defense! Don't give them anything easy. Bear down, Jack. You've got the middle of the order coming up—the 3-4-5 hitters."

Remembering that Stafford's third batter had hit his changeup, Jack started with a fastball. It just missed the outside corner.

Ball one.

Jack came right back with the same pitch. The batter slapped a hard grounder to the Bears second baseman for the first out.

Jack's next fastball flew right over the heart of the plate. The Stafford cleanup batter ripped it down the line for a double.

Come on, hit the corners! Jack told himself. *Stay away from the middle.*

Runner on second base. One out.

Jack threw a fastball to the low outside corner. But this time, the batter was ready. He went with the pitch and smacked a single between the first and second basemen.

The runner on second took off and sprinted all the way home. Now the Bears were behind 1–0.

Runner on first. One out.

Danny stepped in front of home plate, lifted his mask, and shouted encouragement to Jack. "No sweat, buddy! We'll get it back. Get this guy."

But Jack overthrew some fastballs and bounced a changeup, walking his first batter of the game. Now there were runners at first and second, one out.

Jack aimed his next pitch closer to the middle of the plate.

Crack!

Jack turned to see the Bears first baseman dive and knock down the hard-hit grounder. Jack scrambled off the mound to cover first base, and the first baseman flicked him an underhand toss as he ran.

Jack caught the ball midstride and touched the bag a split second before the runner.

The batter was out, but the other two Stafford runners had moved up. Now there were runners at second and third, two outs. A hit could put the Bears behind by three runs—more runs than they could hope to score against Stafford and its ace pitcher in the time left. Jack knew he had to get the next batter.

He stood on the mound as the players on the bench and the fans cheered. Finn's advice came back to him again: *Remember, this is the eighth hitter. He's near the bottom of the order for a reason. Go right after him.*

Jack flooded two fastballs by the Stafford hitter to get ahead in the count—no balls, two strikes. The next pitch flew high and wide. One ball, two strikes. Jack took a deep breath. *Stay on top of it,* he heard Finn say in his head. *Keep the ball low and away.*

Danny flashed a sign for a changeup. Jack shook his head. *Go right after him,* Jack could hear Finn saying.

Jack went into his windup and uncorked

his best fastball. He could almost see it streaking toward the chalked bricks on the school wall. The batter swung. The ball hit Danny's mitt.

"Strike three!" the umpire cried. "You're out!"

The Bears exploded in cheers as they ran off the field.

"Yes! Great pitch."

"Way to go, Jack!"

"Let's get that run back."

The Bears were down by one run, 1–0 after four innings. But they were still in the game.

Jack grabbed his water bottle and dropped down on the Bears bench. "We needed that last out," he said to his friends.

"Yeah," Danny said as he watched the Stafford pitcher warming up on the mound. "We're not going to score a lot off this guy."

Jack leaned over toward Annie. "So...how many pitches?"

Annie pulled the scorebook to her chest. "Give it a break, Jack. You're doing fine." She pointed to the scoreboard. "You're behind 1–0 in the top of the fifth inning. That's all you have to know."

"I just want to see if I'll have a chance to go all seven innings," Jack persisted. "Coach won't leave me in if I throw too many pitches."

Annie lowered the scorebook.

INNING	PITCHES	STRIKES	BALLS	RUNS
1st	ＷＷＩＩ⑫	ＷＩＩＩ⑧	ＩＩＩＩ④	0
2nd	ＷＩＩＩＩ⑨	ＷＩＩ⑦	ＩＩ②	0
3rd	ＷＷ⑩	ＷＩ⑥	ＩＩＩＩ④	0
4th	ＷＷＩＩＩ⑬	ＷＩＩＩ⑧	Ｗ⑤	1
5th				

"You're in good shape," she said. "You've only thrown forty-four pitches. That's an average of eleven per inning."

Jack nodded and did a quick calculation in his head. "If I keep it up, I'll probably go all seven innings."

"*If* you keep it up," Danny said.

Jack stayed solid for the next two innings. He mixed up his pitches, keeping his fastball on the lower outside corner of the plate and coming inside with some pitches to keep the batters off balance. He also threw his changeup every few pitches, especially against the better hitters. Jack realized that, for the first time, he was thinking and really pitching instead of just throwing the ball as fast as he could.

He gave up only one hit, no walks, and no runs in the fifth and sixth innings. The Stafford pitcher was just as good, though. Jaylin managed to rip a line drive between the left and center fielders to start the top of the fifth inning. But the Stafford pitcher settled down and stopped that rally cold.

The Bears were still trailing, 1–0, when they came to bat in the top of the seventh and final inning.

"We're in trouble," Danny said, sitting on the edge of the bench. "We've got the bottom of the order. Our eighth and ninth hitters are starting off the inning."

"Well, don't give up," Annie said. "They might get on."

Jack stood against the chain-link screen and cheered. "Come on, Ben, start us off!" he called to the Bears batter. "Be a base-runner. Walk is as good as a hit. Make it be in there."

The Stafford pitcher, trying to put something extra on his fastball, missed high with his first two pitches. Standing in the third base coach's box, Coach Bentley flashed the take sign, signaling Ben not to swing.

The next pitch was right down the pike. Two balls, one strike. Coach Bentley flashed the take sign again. The pitch was high again. Three balls, one strike.

Coach Bentley clapped his hands. "Be a hitter," he called. The next pitch was close, but Ben held back.

"Ball four," the umpire called. "Take your base."

The leadoff base runner gave the Bears hope. "Walking the leadoff batter is always trouble," Jack muttered, still standing at the screen.

"Hey, trouble for them is good for us," Danny said. He and Jack did a quick fist bump.

The Bears ninth batter plopped down a perfect sacrifice bunt, moving Ben to second base. Now there was a runner at second, one out with Jaylin coming to bat.

The Bears pounded their hands against the dugout screen.

"Come on, Jaylin!"

"Be a hitter."

"Drive him in."

Jaylin let the first two pitches fly by. Two balls, no strikes. Now he was ahead in the count and had the pitcher where he wanted him. Jaylin swung on the next fastball and whacked a hard single to left field.

Sensing the chance for the tying run, Coach Bentley waved Ben home. Ben saw the sign and took off.

The left fielder charged the ball as Ben rounded third. Then Ben turned on the jets and powered toward home. The fielder fired the ball low and hard to the catcher. Ben saw the throw coming in and dropped into a slide. The ball bounced off his leg as he stretched his foot and toed the edge of the plate in a spray of dirt.

"Safe!" the umpire called as the catcher and the pitcher scrambled after the ball.

Jack, Annie, and all the Bears jumped up. Jaylin had passed second base and was motoring toward third. "Go! Go!" they yelled, waving their arms.

The Stafford pitcher scooped up the ball, but it was too late. Jaylin was on third, out of breath but smiling.

The score was tied, 1–1, with a runner at third, one out. The go-ahead run was just 90 feet from home plate. Danny headed to the batter's box. The Bears bench was still on its feet and cheering.

"Come on, Danny! Be a hitter."

The Stafford pitcher fired hard, whipping two straight fastballs by Danny. But the Bears catcher connected on the third pitch and lifted a lazy fly ball down the right field line.

Jack and Annie peered through the chainlink screen, trying to see if the fly ball was fair or foul. The Stafford right fielder straddled the foul line and kept his eyes on the falling ball.

"Jaylin can tag up, even if it's foul," Jack said to Annie. They both looked to third base. Jaylin was standing at the bag, ready to run.

The ball dropped into the fielder's glove in foul territory.

"Go!" shouted Coach Bentley.

Jaylin burst to a sprint and flew across home plate with time to spare.

In a flash, with one hit, some smart baserunning by Jaylin, and a little luck, the Bears had grabbed the lead, 2–1.

Jack ran to the pitcher's mound after the Bears' third out. He was pumped. *They have the bottom of the order coming up,* he reminded himself. *Throw strikes.*

Danny was thinking the same way as he stood with Jack at the pitcher's mound. "They probably won't be swinging on the first pitch," he said. "So put your first pitch right in there. Get ahead in the count."

Jack did just that with the first batter, blistering two fastballs by him. Then he struck him out on a changeup that darted low in the strike zone.

One out.

Stafford sent up a pinch hitter next. Jack kept throwing strikes and got the batter to tap a grounder to shortstop. Jaylin scooped it up and threw to first.

Two outs.

Everyone—both benches and all the fans, including Jack's parents and his sister Sarah—were on their feet.

"Come on, Jack! One more."

"Keep throwing strikes."

"Let's go, Bears! Make a play for him."

Jack could feel a nervous flutter rising in his chest. His first two pitches flew high and wide. Two balls, no strikes.

Come on, don't walk him, Jack scolded himself. *Make him earn it. The top of the order is coming up next. Throw strikes.*

Jack took a deep breath, tugged his cap down along his brow, and remembered what Finn had said: *Go right after those guys at the bottom of the order.* Jack's next two fastballs split the heart of the plate. The count was two balls and two strikes.

Jack just missed with his next pitch. The count was full: three balls, two strikes. Danny set up in the middle of the plate. He knew Jack couldn't afford to give the batter a free pass. Jack went into his windup, trying to do all the things Finn had taught him. The ball flew right for the middle of the plate.

Crack!

Jack turned and saw Ben, the Bears center fielder, run back a few steps and stop. Ben raised his glove and caught the ball easily for the third out.

The Bears had won, 2–1.

They were in the playoffs!

Jack had pitched a complete game.

The Bears ran off the field and celebrated with fist bumps, forearm bumps, and chest bumps. Jack looked up and saw his parents cheering. His father punched the air with a victory fist and his mother was jumping up and down. Sarah cupped her hands around her mouth and shouted, "Great game, little brother! You're awesome!"

Jack couldn't wait to tell Finn.

Thump! Finn dropped the bucket of baseballs beside the pitcher's mound. "So, it
sounds like you pitched a pretty good
game on Tuesday," he said.

Jack had been bursting to tell Finn all
about the game at lunch, but he hadn't been
able to get a word in. Sarah and his mom and
dad and Finn had hogged the conversation
during the entire meal. They always wanted
to talk about work or school or books. Now
Finn was ready to talk about baseball!

"Yeah, I only gave up one run and four hits
in seven innings," Jack bragged as Danny
stood beside him, smiling. "I went all the
way, and Annie said I threw something like
eighty pitches."

"He was amazing," Danny said.

"Did you use the changeup?" Finn asked.

"Yeah, a lot," Jack said. "I mostly threw it to the better hitters. You know, the top and the middle of the order. I went right after the other guys with my fastball, just like you said."

"He started the cleanup hitter with a changeup in the first inning," Danny chimed in. "He totally fooled the guy and got him to ground out to Jaylin."

Finn's eyebrows arched up above his sunglasses. "That's pretty good," he said, nodding. "It makes the other team think you might throw the changeup anytime."

This is the first time I've impressed this guy, Jack thought. *Finally.*

"How many walks did you give up?" Finn asked.

"One," Jack answered proudly.

"Just one?" Finn asked in disbelief.

"One," Jack repeated.

"Well, you're not throwing like Steve Dalkowski anymore," Finn said, with approval. "That's for sure."

"Who's Steve Dalkowski?" Danny asked.

"I'll tell you later," Jack said.

"Who got the hits for the other team?" Finn asked.

"The third hitter got a clean single in the first inning," Jack said as he pulled on his glove. "Then the leadoff guy got a single in one of the early innings. Oh yeah, and I threw a changeup too high to the cleanup hitter. He crushed it for a double."

"Then the fifth hitter went to right field with that fastball you put on the outside corner," Danny said. He jogged backward toward home plate to get into position. "It was like he was waiting for it," he called.

"Sounds like we've got some work to do, then," Finn said.

"A four-hitter is pretty good, isn't it?" Jack said. "I mean, how much better can you do?"

Finn held up both his hands as if he wanted Jack to stop. "Hey, a four-hitter is great," he said. "Especially when you go all seven innings and give up only one walk. But you want to play high school baseball, don't you?"

"Sure," Jack said.

"Me too," Danny called from home plate.

112

"Well, you know those 3-4-5 hitters?" Finn went on. "You'll probably pitch against them in high school." He paused and rubbed his face. "We've got to figure a way to get those guys out, too."

Jack nodded. For the first time he understood what Finn was talking about when he talked about getting better. It meant *always* trying to get better.

"How old are you again?" Finn asked Jack.

"Thirteen."

"When will you be fourteen?"

"In a month or so. On June sixth."

Finn looked Jack up and down, like he was trying to figure how much he weighed or how strong he was. "I'll start showing you how to throw the curveball around your birthday," he said finally. Then his voice turned stern, like a teacher when the class got too loud. "But I don't want you throwing it a lot. I just want you to get a feel for it."

Jack could barely hold back his excitement. "Didn't Koufax have a good curveball?" he asked.

"He had a *great* curveball," Finn corrected.

"A real hammer. They say it dropped a foot." He looked at Jack. "I'll show it to you...later."

Finn leaned over and picked a couple of baseballs out of the bucket. "Until then, let's work on locating the fastball on the inside corner, too," he said. "So guys like that fifth batter won't always be looking for your fastball on the *outside* corner." He turned toward Danny. "Give him a good target on the inside corner," he said.

Danny did as he was told. He pulled down his mask and got into his catcher's stance, his mitt hovering over the razor's edge of the inside corner of the plate.

Finn flipped Jack a baseball. Jack stood on the pitcher's mound for a minute, feeling the sun beat down on the back of his neck with the promise of summer and more baseball games. Then he leaned over and focused on Danny's mitt.

Somehow, with Finn standing there near the mound, the target didn't seem so small or so far away anymore. In fact, as Jack went into his pitching motion, Danny's glove looked big—almost close.

Closer than 60 feet 6 inches away. Bigger than the two bricks Finn had chalked on the side of the school all that time ago.

Bigger and closer than ever before.

The Real Story

When Steve Dalkowski pitched in the 1950s and 1960s, baseball coaches and scouts didn't have pitch-speed guns like they do today. So no one knows for sure how fast Dalkowski's famous fastball really was.

But the story goes that Hall of Fame slugger Ted Williams once declared that Dalkowski was "the fastest ever." Baltimore Orioles managers Earl Weaver and Cal Ripken Sr. both claimed that Dalkowski threw harder than Hall of Fame pitcher and career strikeout leader Nolan Ryan. Other baseball experts estimated that Dalkowski threw the ball as fast as 105 miles an hour. (An average major league fastball goes "only" 90 miles an hour.)

A look at Dalkowski's pitching career indicates that the 5-foot-11-inch, 170-pound left-hander from New Britain, Connecticut, must have thrown the baseball extremely hard. For example, in high school Dalkowski once struck out twenty-four batters in a single game. That is still a record for Connecticut high schools.

The Baltimore Orioles signed Dalkowski in 1957 and assigned him to its minor league system. If he did well in the minor leagues, he would become a major league pitcher for the Baltimore Orioles. In his first year as a minor leaguer, Dalkowski racked up amazing strikeout totals. In one game, he again struck out twenty-four batters—but that feat was a lot harder in the minor leagues than it had been in high school.

Baseball is a game of statistics, and Dalkowski's pitching stats are incredible. He pitched 180 innings in his first two seasons of minor league ball, striking out 353 batters. That means Dalkowski struck out almost two batters every inning during those first two seasons. No wonder they called him

"White Lightning." Even the greatest strike-out pitchers, such as Nolan Ryan, Randy Johnson, and Roger Clemens, average only one strikeout for every inning they pitch.

Batters couldn't touch Dalkowski's blazing fastball. The hitters managed only seventy-five hits during Dalkowski's first 180 innings. So Dalkowski gave up only one hit every two or three innings. Good pitchers give up about one hit every inning.

The problem was that Dalkowski walked as many batters as he struck out. In that minor league game in which he struck out twenty-four batters, he walked eighteen batters and hit four others with pitches. Dalkowski's team lost that game, 8–4.

And even though he whiffed so many batters in his first two seasons in minor league ball, Dalkowski walked even more—an unbelievable 374 batters in 180 innings!

The Orioles coaches hoped that Dalkowski would settle down and find the plate. But his wild ways continued. In 1960 Dalkowski pitched 170 innings and gave up only 105 hits. He struck out 262 batters. But he walked the exact same number. His record for the year was seven wins and fifteen losses.

In 1962, he started to improve—he only walked 114 batters in 160 innings. But he hurt his arm early in 1963 and his legendary speedball was gone. He never made it to the major leagues and dropped out of baseball after the 1965 season.

Another pitching phenom who had control problems at the beginning of his career was Sandy Koufax. The left-hander from Brooklyn, New York, was drafted in 1954 by the Brooklyn Dodgers (which later became the Los Angeles Dodgers). He was so talented that the Dodgers started him right off as a major league pitcher instead of assigning him to its minor league system.

Koufax threw hard, but he was too wild to have much success. In his first six seasons with the Dodgers, Koufax pitched 691 innings and walked 405 batters. That's not as bad as Dalkowski, but it is still too many to be a dependable major league pitcher. In fact, Koufax's win-loss record for those first six seasons was 36–40. That was hardly Hall of Fame material.

But things changed dramatically during a spring training game in 1961. The Dodgers had brought only part of their team to the game. Without a full roster of pitchers, Koufax was scheduled to pitch at least seven innings.

Koufax got off to a terrible start. He was even wilder than usual and he walked the first three batters. With the bases loaded, the Dodgers catcher, Norm Sherry, visited Koufax on the mound. "Take something off the ball and let 'em hit it," Sherry told the young pitcher. "Nobody's going to swing the way you're throwing now."

Koufax took his catcher's advice. As he said later, he "took the grunt out of every pitch." In other words, he didn't try to throw every pitch as hard as he could. Instead, he concentrated on throwing the ball over the plate and he quit worrying about whether the batter hit the ball or not.

The change was immediate. Koufax struck out the next three batters. For the seven innings he pitched, he didn't give up a hit. He struck out eight batters and, most importantly, only walked another two. Koufax wrote later, "I came home a different pitcher than the one who had left."

The future Hall of Famer was on his way. The 1961 season was his best yet: he won eighteen games and walked only ninety-six batters in more than 255 innings.

With his blazing fastball and amazing curveball under control, Koufax kept getting better. For the five seasons from 1962 to 1966, Koufax was perhaps the greatest pitcher who ever lived. He threw four no-hitters, including a perfect game (no one got on base: no hits and no walks). He won three Cy Young awards for being the best pitcher in both the National and American Leagues. He led the National League in earned run average (ERA) for five straight seasons—something no pitcher has done, either before or since.

Sandy Koufax had learned what Finn taught Jack in the story—and what, sadly,

Steve Dalkowski never learned. It is more important that a pitcher throw strikes than throw the ball fast. No pitcher can be a winner if he walks too many batters. There is much more to pitching than just throwing heat!

Acknowledgments

Much of the information about Steve Dalkowski came from Wikipedia and the book FROM 33RD STREET TO CAMDEN YARDS: AN ORAL HISTORY OF THE BALTIMORE ORIOLES by John Eisenberg (McGraw-Hill, 2002 paperback edition).

The information about Sandy Koufax came from the book SANDY KOUFAX: A LEFTY'S LEGACY by Jane Leavy (HarperCollins, 2002), as well as the article "The Left Arm of God" by Tom Verducci, which appeared in *Sports Illustrated* on July 12, 1999, and was anthologized in SPORTS ILLUSTRATED'S GREAT BASEBALL WRITING (2005).

The statistics for the players are from the indispensable baseball website: *www.baseball-reference.com*.

The author thanks his son Liam Bowen, the pitching coach at St. Mary's College in Maryland, for his help with the technical aspects of pitching, and Nadia Abouraya for her help in typing the original manuscript.

About the Author

Fred Bowen was a Little Leaguer who loved to read. Now he is the author of many action-packed books of sports fiction. He has also written a weekly sports column for kids in the *Washington Post* since 2000.

For thirteen years, Fred coached kids' baseball and basketball teams. Some of his stories spring directly from his coaching experience and his sports-happy childhood in Marblehead, Massachusetts.

Fred holds a degree in history from the University of Pennsylvania and a law degree from George Washington University. He was a lawyer for many years before retiring to become a full-time children's author. Bowen has been a guest author at schools and conferences across the country, as well as the Smithsonian Institute in Washington, DC, and The Baseball Hall of Fame.

Fred lives in Silver Spring, Maryland, with his wife Peggy Jackson. Their son is a college baseball coach and their daughter is a college student.

For more information
check out the author's website.
www.fredbowen.com

ley, sports fans!

Don't miss all the action-packed books by Fred Bowen.
Check out www.SportsStorySeries.com for more info.

Dugout Rivals
PB: $5.95 / 978-1-56145-515-7 / 1-56145-515-6

Last year Jake was one of his team's best players. But this season it looks like a new kid is going to take Jake's place as team leader. Can Jake settle for second-best?

Hardcourt Comeback
PB: $5.95 / 978-1-56145-516-4 / 1-56145-516-4

Brett blew a key play in an important game. Now he feels like a loser for letting his teammates down—and he keeps making mistakes. How can Brett become a "winner" again?

Soccer Team Upset
PB: $5.95 / 978-1-56145-495-2 / 1-56145-495-8

Tyler is angry when his team's star player leaves to join an elite travel team. Just as Tyler expected, the Cougars' season goes straight downhill. Can he make a difference before it's too late?

Touchdown Trouble
PB: $5.95 / 978-1-56145-497-6 / 1-56145-497-4

Thanks to a major play by Sam, the Cowboys beat their arch rivals to remain undefeated. But the celebration ends when Sam and his teammates make an unexpected discovery. Is their perfect season in jeopardy?

Throwing Heat
PB: $5.95 / 978-1-56145-540-9 / 1-56145-540-7

Jack throws the fastest pitches around, but lately his blazing fastballs haven't been enough. He's got to learn new pitches to stay ahead of the batters. But can he resist bringing the heat?

Want more?
All-St⭐r Sports Story
Series

T. J.'s Secret Pitch
PB: $5.95 / 978-1-56145-504-1 / 1-56145-504-0

T. J.'s pitches just don't pack the power they need to strike out the batters, but the story of 1940s baseball hero Rip Sewell and his legendary eephus pitch may help him find a solution.

The Golden Glove
PB: $5.95 / 978-1-56145-505-8 / 1-56145-505-9

Without his lucky glove, Jamie doesn't believe in his ability to lead his baseball team to victory, until he learns that faith in oneself is the most important equipment for any game.

The Kid Coach
PB: $5.95 / 978-1-56145-506-5 / 1-56145-506-7

Scott and his teammates can't find an adult to coach their team, so they must find a leader among themselves.

Playoff Dreams
PB: $5.95 / 978-1-56145-507-2 / 1-56145-507-5

Brendan is one of the best players in the league, but no matter how hard he tries, he can't make his team win.

Winners Take All
PB: $5.95 / 978-1-56145-512-6 / 1-56145-512-1

Kyle makes a poor decision to cheat in a big game. Someone discovers the truth and threatens to reveal it. What can Kyle do now?

All-Star Sports Story series

Want more?

All-St★r Sports Story Series

Full Court Fever

PB: $5.95 / 978-1-56145-508-9 / 1-56145-508-3

The Falcons have the skill but not the height to win their games. Will the full-court zone press be the solution to their problem?

Off the Rim

PB: $5.95 / 978-1-56145-509-6 / 1-56145-509-1

Hoping to be more than a benchwarmer, Chris learns that defense is just as important as offense.

The Final Cut

PB: $5.95 / 978-1-56145-510-2 / 1-56145-510-5

ur friends realize that they may not all make the team and that the tryouts are a test—not only of their athletic skills, but of their friendship as well.

On the Line

PB: $5.95 / 978-1-56145-511-9 / 1-56145-511-3

Marcus is the highest scorer and the best rebounder, but e's not so great at free throws—until the school custodian helps him overcome his fear of failure.

All-Star Sports Story series

C.Lit PZ 7 .B6724 Th 2010
Bowen, Fred.
Throwing heat